A guide to the meaning and
pronunciation of some dinosaur names printed
in **bold** can be found in the glossary.

Acknowledgments

The publishers would like to thank Wendy Body for acting as
reading level consultant and the British Museum of Natural
History for advising on scientific content.

Photographic credits

Pages 36 and 39, G. S. F. Picture Library; pages 40 and 41 bottom,
The Mansell Collection; page 41 top, Ann Ronan Picture Library;
page 43, The British Museum of Natural History.

Ladybird books are widely available, but in case of
difficulty may be ordered by post or telephone from:

Ladybird Books – Cash Sales Department
Littlegate Road Paignton Devon TQ3 3BE
Telephone 0803 554761

A catalogue record for this book is available
from the British Library

Published by Ladybird Books Ltd Loughborough Leicestershire UK
Ladybird Books Inc Auburn Maine 04210 USA

© LADYBIRD BOOKS LTD 1994

Dinosaurs

written by BRIDGET DALY
and MICHAEL WOODS
illustrated by CHRIS FORSEY

What were the dinosaurs?

Millions of years ago, long before there were people on Earth, some extraordinary creatures roamed our planet. They were *reptiles*, like crocodiles and lizards. Some of these reptiles swam in the sea or flew in the air. But one special kind, the *dinosaurs*, ruled on land. Their reign lasted for 160 million years.

Why 'dinosaur'?

The word 'dinosaur' was invented by the English scientist Richard Owen in 1841. It means 'terrible lizard' in Greek.

There were many different kinds of dinosaurs. Some of them were giant, peaceful plant-eaters...

...and some dinosaurs had deadly slashing teeth and claws, which they used to kill and eat other reptiles.

5

The age of dinosaurs

The world looked quite different
when dinosaurs first appeared

Development of animals time chart

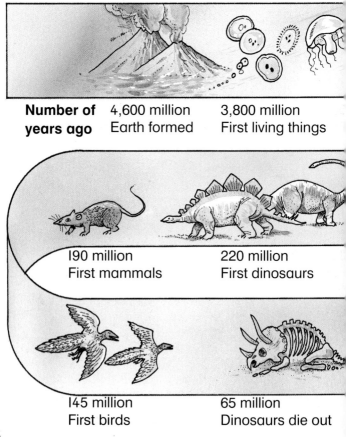

Number of years ago	4,600 million Earth formed	3,800 million First living things
	190 million First mammals	220 million First dinosaurs
	145 million First birds	65 million Dinosaurs die out

on Earth, about 220 million years ago. There were no buildings and no roads and no humans. The weather was very warm all year.

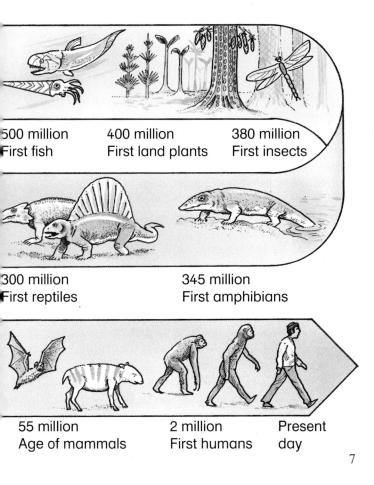

500 million
First fish

400 million
First land plants

380 million
First insects

300 million
First reptiles

345 million
First amphibians

55 million
Age of mammals

2 million
First humans

Present day

Dinosaur ancestors

The first ancestors of the dinosaurs were fish called *lobefins*. Gradually, they began to pull themselves out of the water and onto the land. Over millions of years, the first *amphibians* developed.

Eusthenopteron was a lobefin about 1 m long. It was a fierce, bony freshwater fish. It had strong muscles in its fins to support it on land. It had lungs as well as gills so it could stay out of water and breathe air for short periods.

Amphibians were halfway between fish and land animals, like the frogs, toads and newts of today. They could live on land part of the time.

Ichthyostega was one of the first amphibians. It had lungs and proper legs and feet. But it had to return to water to keep its skin wet and to lay its eggs.

From amphibians to reptiles

Amphibians could live on dry land but they had to stay near water. Slowly, over millions of years, some kinds of amphibians developed into reptiles. Reptiles could live on land all the time. They had scaly, waterproof skins to stop them drying out and their eggs had tough shells to protect them.

Seymouria

The secret of the reptiles' success was their eggs. Amphibians' eggs are small and soft, like frogspawn. They dry up and die if they are left out of water.

Reptiles' eggs have a tough, waterproof shell, which does not dry out. Safe inside the shell, the young reptile is fed by a large supply of yolk until it hatches.

Hylonomus

It is difficult to tell the difference between this small early reptile, **Hylonomus**, and this amphibian, **Seymouria**. But Hylonomus had a thicker, scaly skin to protect it from damage and the drying sun and wind.

The first dinosaurs

Dinosaurs probably developed from a type of reptile called a *thecodont*, which was something like a crocodile. But unlike crocodiles, dinosaurs held their legs under their bodies. Some could run fast on their back legs, using their tails to balance. Other large, heavy creatures walked on two or four legs.

Coelophysis was a light and speedy meat-eating dinosaur. It had clawed 'hands' and many small, sharp teeth. It is seen here with a small plant-eating dinosaur called **Heterodontosaurus**.

Reptiles such as lizards waddle along on bent, sprawling legs.

Thecodonts held their legs further under their bodies.

Dinosaurs' legs were tucked well under their bodies, supporting their weight. This meant they could stand taller and run faster.

13

All shapes and sizes

Scientists have discovered over 800 species of dinosaurs. Over the millions of years that they roamed Earth, dinosaurs developed in many different ways to suit the changing conditions on Earth. **Mamenchisaurus** was as long as four buses parked in a row but **Compsognathus** was no bigger than a chicken.

Compsognathus was 60 cm long and a fast-running meat-eater.

Stegosaurus was 7 m long but had a brain the size of a walnut.

The largest dinosaur
footprints ever found
were so enormous that
they could hold as
much water as a bath.
They were found in
Texas, USA.

Triceratops was 9 m
long. Its fearsome
horns could be at
least a metre long.

Mamenchisaurus
was 22 m long, 4 m
high and weighed
about 30 tonnes.

15

Gentle giants

The largest dinosaurs were called *sauropods*. They had huge bodies, long necks and even longer tails. But they were very slow and had tiny brains. They could feed only on soft plants as their teeth were weak and stumpy. They needed to eat a huge amount to keep themselves alive and had enormous stomachs.

Diplodocus was the longest land animal ever known. Its neck was 8 m long, its body 5 m and its tail a massive 14 m.

This dinosaur skull shows that plant-eating dinosaurs had small even teeth, rather like this giraffe's front teeth. They were used for stripping leaves off plants.

dinosaur

giraffe

Brachiosaurus

Diplodocus

Eating the highest leaves is **Brachiosaurus**. It weighed 80 tonnes, more than fifteen elephants. Its very long front legs gave it extra height.

Monster meat-eaters

Not all dinosaurs ate plants.
Many fed on other dinosaurs or
smaller reptiles, snails or insects.
Some hunted together in packs or
groups. They were small and fast,
with slashing teeth and claws.
Others were slow, bulky monsters
whose huge jaws could bite into
dinosaurs with thick,
tough skins.

Deinonychus
was the fiercest, fastest flesh-eater. It
slashed its prey with its huge razor-sharp
second claw, which was 12 cm long.

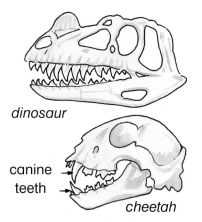

dinosaur

canine
teeth →

cheetah

The skull of a meat-eating dinosaur had long sharp teeth, like steak knives, for tearing flesh. See how the shape of the teeth are quite like the canine teeth of a cheetah.

Megalosaurus was the first dinosaur to be given a name. It weighed 9 tonnes. Like many large meat-eaters, it had a solid, bulky shape.

19

Dinosaurs in armour

The big, slow plant-eaters could not escape easily from their enemies. Some of them, called *ankylosaurs*, had heavy bony plates and spines over their backs and tails. These protected them from attack, like a suit of armour.

The back of **Euoplocephalus** was completely covered with bony lumps and spikes and a leathery skin. Its head had a 'helmet' of hard plates. Even its eyelids had bony coverings.

Paleoscincus had a heavy body and short legs. A fringe of sharp spikes stuck out all round the edge of its armour.

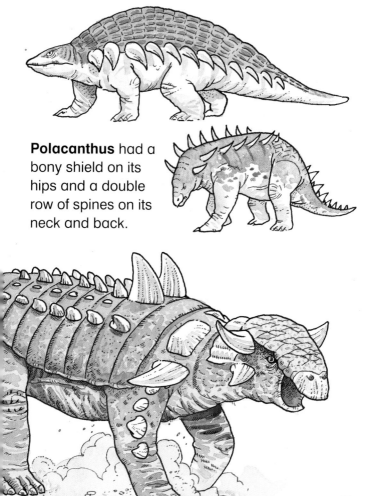

Polacanthus had a bony shield on its hips and a double row of spines on its neck and back.

A herd of three-horned **Triceratops** surrounds an attacking **Tyrannosaurus**. Even a fierce killer like this would probably have run away when faced with those horns.

Great defenders

Some dinosaurs looked rather like our modern rhinos. They had sharp horns to defend themselves and a bony frill to protect their necks. They were all plant-eaters and their hugely strong jaws could have tackled very tough food.

Protoceratops was a small, horned dinosaur. It was one of the first of this group and had only bony lumps, not true horns.

Lumps, bumps and crests

The oddest shaped heads in the dinosaur kingdom belonged to duckbilled dinosaurs called *hadrosaurs*. Their lumps, bumps and crests were mostly hollow and joined to the air-holes in their noses. But no one knows what they were for, although there are several ideas.

Parasaurolophus had a crest 2 m long, the size of a man! Perhaps it was used to push aside undergrowth as the animal moved along.

Tsintaosaurus had a hollow horn on its forehead that may have been used like a trumpet.

Pachycephalosaurus was not a hadrosaur but it also had a strange head. The dome on top was about 25 cm thick. It may have had head-butting contests to see who should be leader of the herd.

The smallest dinosaurs

We often think of dinosaurs as huge monsters but there were some that were only the size of a hen or duck.

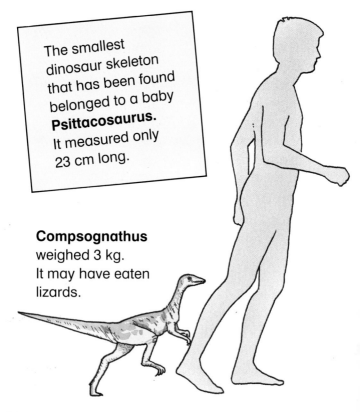

The smallest dinosaur skeleton that has been found belonged to a baby **Psittacosaurus.** It measured only 23 cm long.

Compsognathus weighed 3 kg. It may have eaten lizards.

These creatures were light and quick. They could pounce on small prey or run away into the undergrowth or into a crack in the rocks to escape from their enemies.

Lesothosaurus was 90 cm long and ran on its long back legs. It had a horny 'beak' and probably fed on leaves and shoots.

Saltopus was a slim and speedy little meat-eating dinosaur. It was 90 cm long and weighed only about 1 kg. It probably ate insects.

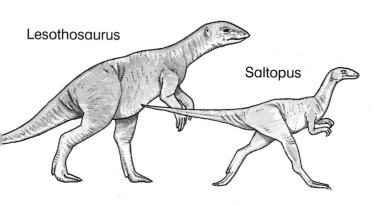

Lesothosaurus

Saltopus

Pteranodon had a long, toothless beak which it used to snatch fish from the sea. It stored them in a pouch under its beak.

The small and agile **Pterodactylus** spent most of its time in the air, like a swallow, snapping insects as it flew. It probably hung upside down to rest, like a bat.

The largest animal ever to fly was **Quetzalcoatlus** with a wingspan of 12 m. It was the size of a two-seater aircraft.

Flying reptiles

Dinosaurs could not fly, but some reptiles, called *pterosaurs*, could. They ruled the skies for almost as long as the dinosaurs ruled the land. Pterosaurs were more like bats than birds. Their wings were made of leathery skin stretched between their long arms and back legs.

Sea reptiles

Throughout the age of the dinosaurs, the oceans were filled with reptiles. Some looked like sea serpents, with long snake-like necks that reared out of the water. Others looked like crocodiles or dolphins. They all breathed air and came to the water's surface to breathe.

Ichthyosaurus was a dolphin-like reptile with a tail like a fish and flippers. It hunted in packs and ate squid and fish.

Elasmosaurus had
a neck 6 m long, the
same length as its
body. It flapped its
flippers up and down
like a turtle.

Metriorhynchus was a fish-like crocodile.
It had a tail flipper, webbed hands and feet,
and very sharp teeth.

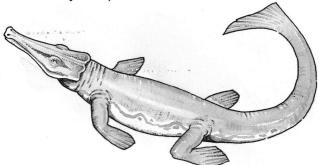

The most famous dinosaur of all

Perhaps the best known dinosaur of all is **Tyrannosaurus**. Poor duckbilled dinosaurs stood no chance against the large jaws and tearing teeth of such a huge and frightening monster.

Its jaws were 1.5 m long with huge 15 cm saw-like teeth. It tore off lumps of flesh and swallowed them whole.

The massive tail was used to balance the weight of its body and heavy head.

Tyrannosaurus was the largest known meat-eating animal ever to live on land. It was 5 m tall, 14 m long and weighed 7 tonnes.

It walked on its powerful back legs, moving at about 4 km an hour, the speed of a walking human. No one knows how it used its tiny two-clawed hands.

The end of the dinosaurs

About 65 million years ago, the dinosaurs and all their large reptile relatives died within quite a short space of time. No one knows for sure why this happened but different ideas have been suggested.

Towards the end of the age of the dinosaurs many small mammals lived on Earth. Could they have stolen and eaten too many of the dinosaurs' eggs?

Perhaps Earth was struck by a huge meteorite. Dust thrown up might have blotted out the Sun so that no plants could grow. Many animals would have starved to death.

Over thousands of years Earth had become colder. The huge reptiles had no fur or feathers to keep them warm. Perhaps they froze to death.

A story in stone

If there are no dinosaurs alive today, how do we know so much about them? We know because we have found their bones, claws, teeth, eggs and footprints, which over millions of years have hardened into rock. They have become fossils. Fossils may be found by miners or builders or if the rock is worn away by wind and rain.

Not only bones become fossilised. These dinosaur footprints were made long ago in soft ground that later hardened to become rock.

When this dinosaur died, it fell to the bottom of a lake. All the soft parts of its body rotted away. Only its skeleton was left.

Over many years, layers of mud covered the bones. The mud around the skeleton slowly hardened into rock. In time the skeleton, too, decayed.

Tiny pieces of rock, called minerals, were washed into the spaces left by the dinosaur's bones. They hardened into fossils.

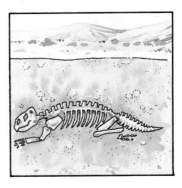

Finding dinosaurs

Sometimes fossilised bones are found lying on the ground. Usually they are still buried, with one or two bones sticking out of the side of a cliff or quarry. The place where the bones are found is called a dig. Scientists carefully remove the bones and take them away to be rebuilt into a dinosaur.

The fossil hunter chips away at the rock around the bone. Then he uses small chisels and brushes to clear away the rest of the rock.

Some fossils are weak and crumbly. They are covered with plaster-soaked bandages that harden as they dry. These protect the fossils so that they can be taken away.

Before each fossil is removed, it is photographed and labelled so that the bones can be put in the right order when the dinosaur is rebuilt.

Assembling a dinosaur is like doing a huge jigsaw puzzle. It often takes months or even years to do.

Dinosaur detectives

For hundreds of years people have been finding fossilised bones. But it is less than two hundred years since scientists first started to study them properly.

In the early 1820s Dr Gideon Mantell and his wife Mary found some dinosaur teeth and bones in Sussex, England. Mantell named the dinosaur **Iguanodon** as its teeth were like an iguana's.

Othniel Marsh, who lived one hundred years ago, was a famous dinosaur detective who made many finds in North America.

'Fossil hunts' were popular a hundred years ago. This old newspaper picture shows one such dig in the Rocky Mountains, USA, in 1878.

Recent discoveries

New dinosaur fossils are being discovered all the time. Each new find gives scientists a better idea of what life was like on Earth all those millions of years ago. Who knows what other exciting discoveries may be made this year?

Ultrasaurus was an enormous plant-eating dinosaur. Its skeleton was found in 1979. Scientists think that it was taller than a five-storey building.

In 1983 William Walker, an English fossil hunter, found a huge claw in a Surrey quarry. Three van loads of bones were taken away to be rebuilt into a huge dinosaur, which was nicknamed 'Claws'.

'Claws' was a new species of meat-eating dinosaur. It was later named **Baryonyx walkeri**. Its famous claw was 30 cm long. It may have been used to hook fish out of the water.

Glossary of some dinosaur names in this book

Baryonyx walkeri
barri-on-iks war-ker-ry
(heavy claw)

Brachiosaurus
bra-kee-o-sor-uss
(arm reptile)

Coelophysis
see-lo-fy-siss
(hollow face)

Compsognathus
komp-sog-nay-thuss
(pretty jaw)

Deinonychus
dy-no-ny-kuss
(terrible claw)

Diplodocus
dip-plod-o-kuss
(double beam)

Euoplocephalus
u-o-plo-keff-al-uss
(true plated head)

Heterodontosaurus
het-ter-o-don-toe-sor-uss
(mixed-tooth reptile)

Iguanodon
ig-wan-o-don
(iguana tooth)

Lesothosaurus
less-o-toe-sor-uss
(reptile from Lesotho)

Mamenchisaurus
ma-men-chee-sor-uss
(reptile from China)

Megalosaurus
meg-a-loss-a-russ
(giant reptile)

Pachycephalosaurus
pak-ee-keff-al-o-sor-uss
(thick-headed reptile)

Paleoscincus
pay-lee-o-skin-kuss
(ancient skink)

Parasaurolophus
pa-ra-sor-rollo-fuss
(reptile with a parallel-sided crest)

Polacanthus
poll-a-kan-thuss
(many spined)

Protoceratops
pro-toe-sair-a-tops
(first horned face)

Psittacosaurus
si-ta-co-sor-uss
(parrot reptile)

Saltopus
sol-toe-puss
(leaping foot)

Stegosaurus
steg-o-sor-russ
(roofed reptile)

Triceratops
try-ser-a-tops
(three-horned face)

Tsintaosaurus
sin-toe-sor-uss
(reptile from Tsintao)

Tyrannosaurus
ty-ran-no-sor-uss
(tyrant reptile)

Ultrasaurus
ull-tra-sor-uss
(largest reptile)